Katinka's Tail

Judith Kerr

HarperCollins *Children's Books*

For Ann-Janine,
with love and thanks

First published in hardback in Great Britain
by HarperCollins Children's Books in 2017

10 9 8 7 6 5 4 3 2 1

ISBN: 978-0-00-825529-9

HarperCollins Children's Books is a division of HarperCollins Publishers Ltd.

Text and illustrations copyright © Kerr-Kneale Productions Ltd 2017

Visit our website at www.harpercollins.co.uk

Printed and bound in China

MIX
Paper from
responsible sources
FSC® C007454

FSC is a non-profit international organisation established to promote the
responsible management of the world's forests. Products carrying the FSC
label are independently certified to assure consumers that they come
from forests that are managed to meet the social, economic and
ecological needs of present and future generations.

Find out more about HarperCollins and the environment at
www.harpercollins.co.uk/green

This is my cat Katinka.
She is a lovely, perfectly ordinary pussycat.

People always notice Katinka.

Then some say, "That tail is really magic."

They say, "Look at that cat with the funny tail."

Others say, "What a peculiar cat. Is she peculiar in other ways too?" This makes me very cross, and I say, "She's just a lovely, perfectly ordinary pussycat."

First thing every morning
Katinka climbs up the
creeper…

to my bedroom window…

and when I draw back the curtains, there she is!

Sometimes she has been playing in the woods, and she is a bit grubby. Then I give her a nice brush.

But she won't let me brush her tail.

She knows that her tail is special.

She likes to help
me get dressed,

and always checks
my shoes for spiders.

Then we go down
to the kitchen.

Sometimes there is a dead
mouse on the floor…

or half a dead mouse.

I throw them out when Katinka isn't looking.

Then I give Katinka her breakfast.

But…

sometimes Katinka thinks my breakfast
looks more interesting.

Sometimes Katinka walks
up the road with me.

She plays in the
woods while I
go to the shops.

But she is always there to meet me
when I come home…

and we unpack the shopping together.

Sometimes
Katinka does
a funny trick.
She lies on
the table.

Then she leans
over the edge…

and a bit more…

and a bit more…

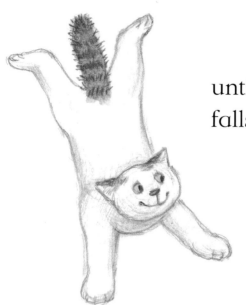

until she
falls off.

Then I say,
"Oh, what a
clever pussycat!"
and she is
very pleased.

One night Katinka and I had
our supper.

Then I put her to bed in her basket...

and went to bed myself.

But in the middle of the night
I woke up with a big sneeze.

So I went downstairs
for some tissues.
Katinka's basket
was empty.

But then I saw her.
She was running,
and there was
something wrong
with her tail.

And the street was full of animals,
running after her.

And when they got to the woods, they all
disappeared, and I was alone in the dark.
But then I noticed a glow behind some trees,
and you'll never believe what I saw.
I shouted, "Katinka! What on earth are you
doing? Whatever are you doing with your tail?"

But Katinka just smiled and went on waving her tail, and then she suddenly floated up in the air, and so did all the animals, and so did I!

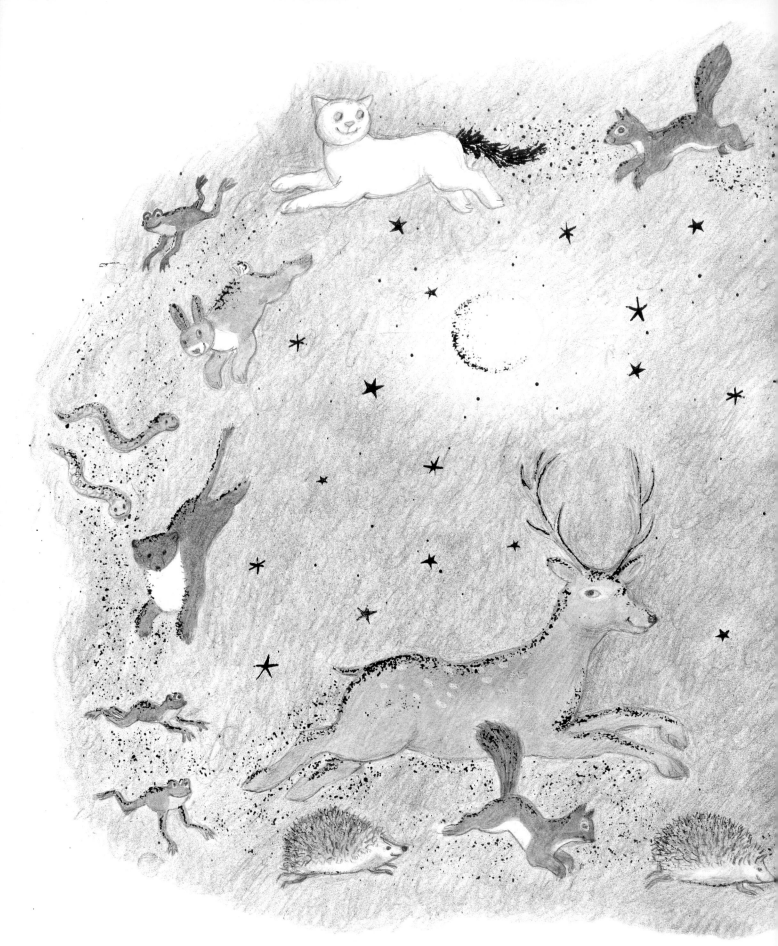

And we floated up through the clouds to the sky above,

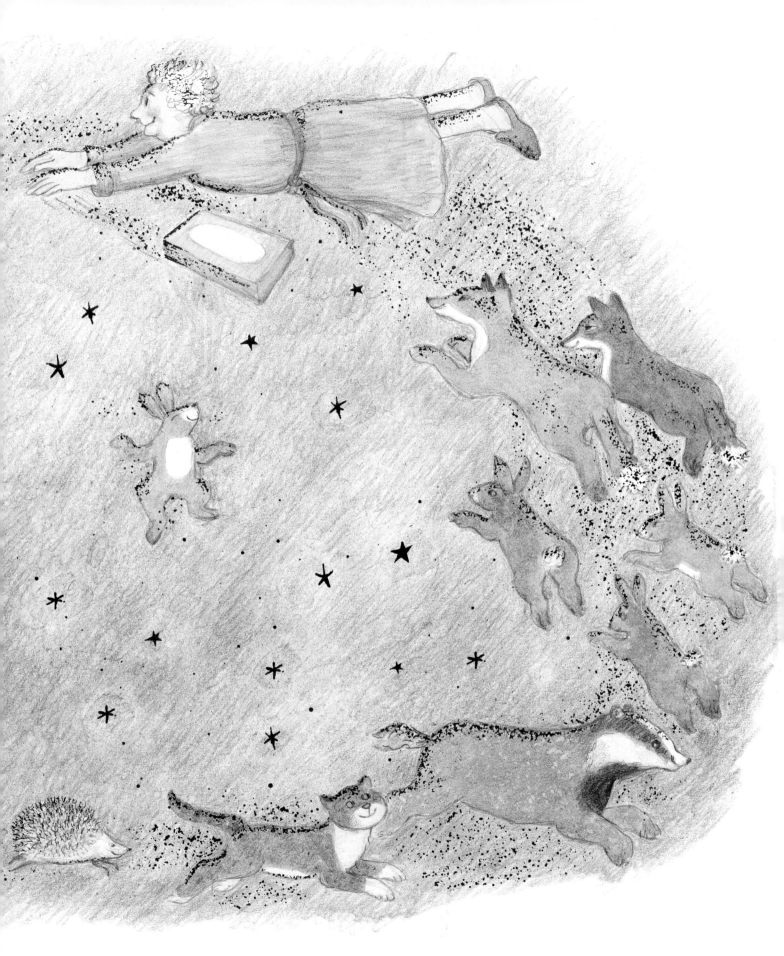

and we flew round and round among the stars.

And then Katinka and I flew to
the moon…

and Katinka caught a
moon mouse and ate it.

And then I flew
back into my
bedroom,

and in the morning I woke up in my bed,
just as usual.
I thought, "What an amazing dream. I must
tell Katinka what I dreamt about her."

So I drew back the curtains, and there she was.
And I said, "Oh!"
Now, when people ask me about Katinka, I say,
"She's a lovely, perfectly ordinary pussycat."
And then I say, "Except, of course, for her tail."